I0529662

The Virgin and the Playboy

A 1Night Stand Story

By
Kate Richards

This book is a work of fiction. Names, characters, places, and incidents are the products of the author's imagination or used fictitiously. Any resemblance to actual events, locales or persons, living or dead, is entirely coincidental.

Published by
Decadent Publishing Company, LLC

Look for us online at:
www.decadentpublishing.com

~What Others Are Saying~

Dedication

Thanks to Valerie Mann and Olivia Starke, co-developers of this idea, and great and loyal friends.

Chapter One

Julia drew a deep breath and looked around the lobby. This was not only her first trip to Las Vegas, it was going to be her first time— well, her *first time*. She had managed to make it all the way through college without losing her virginity, and she was sick to death of waiting around for that perfect guy, that prince charming, to give her innocence to as though it were a wrapped present. Finally time to join the rest of the world and take advantage of the sexual revolution. Her heart threatening to hammer its way out of her chest, she clutched the strap of her overnight bag with a sweaty palm and headed toward the registration desk.

Finding 1NightStand online had been like a dream come true. She could fly to Las Vegas, spend one night with a complete stranger, lose that troublesome membrane and come back caught up with everyone else. Ready to have ordinary dates and hop from bed to bed at will, as all her girlfriends seemed to do. Decision made, she contacted Madame Evangeline and provided the required information and her American Express card number. All the arrangements were made. Julia Hooper, virgin at large, was about to give up what had become most inconvenient and embarrassing—her hymen.

***

In the room only fifteen minutes, Mark had already paced back and forth so many times he could see a pattern of his steps in the freshly vacuumed carpet. He couldn't even believe he was here, about to spend the night with a woman he'd never met. What if she was a dog? Okay, that sounded bad, but still...

His buddies had been merciless in their insistence he try out 1NightStand. It was his own fault—his bragging about dating a different woman every week was probably over the top. When he didn't want to sign up, the guys dared him. He hadn't ever been able to refuse a challenge, and they all knew it, damn them. But he figured once the beer wore off, they would see how ridiculous the whole idea was and let him off the hook.

Not.

If anything, they were more persistent the next day, excited and planning the whole thing. He could barely stop them from coming to Las Vegas with him. Finally, his oath to cancel the whole thing had made them back off and promise to wait back in Los Angeles for his return.

After some more persuading from the guys, he'd decided to go ahead and meet the girl. If she looked like Frankenstein, he would just have to make the best of it and try not to gag. He faced a lot of pressure being the playboy in the group, the single dude who dated all the hot women. Those guys hung on his stories, and he liked seeing the envy in their eyes. It wasn't his fault they'd all let themselves get tied down. Although he was fond of their wives—lovely, sweet women who fed him home-cooked meals and tried to set him up with their friends—he couldn't imagine picking only one woman from the hundreds crowding the clubs. At least not for longer than a week or two.

So, with his usual strut, he'd boarded the plane and wound up in a luxury hotel room on the penthouse floor of a Las Vegas casino. Pacing back and forth, he stared at the door. Any minute now, she would be here. Dear God, what had he been thinking?

***

Julia approached the desk and waited while the desk clerk finished checking in an older couple wearing matching Hawaiian shirts.

"May I help you?"

She scanned the young man's face—was he aware of the nature of her visit?

"Yes, I need Sam Adams's room number please." Julia's voice cracked, her nerves raw.

"Oh, you must be Miss Ross? Betsy Ross?" He looked down at his monitor, and back up at her, his expression pleasant, non-judgmental, she decided. "Mr. Adams is expecting you in Penthouse 4."

Why had the first flag maker's name seemed like a good pseudonym to give for the check-in? Her cheeks flooded with heat. That's what she got for watching *Notting Hill* the night she made the reservation. Using a famous historical figure's name for anonymity, as Julia Roberts had in the film, had sounded dramatic and fun...and apparently her date had felt the same. What had Madame Eve said his name really was? Oh, right. Mark.

"Thank you." She accepted the card key the clerk handed her and turned to look for the bank of elevators. She saw one way at the other end of the casino and another set nearer to where she stood. Which one?

A tall man passing by stopped beside her, smiling. "Are you lost?"

"I'm afraid I am," she said, her cheeks flushing under his dark-eyed regard. Was this good-looking guy her date? It would be too good to be true.

"I'm with the hotel," he said, his pleasant expression giving nothing away. "What can we do to make your stay more enjoyable?"

"Direct me to the penthouse elevator?"

He took her arm and turned her to face the closer set of elevators. "Right over there. You'll need to use your card key to get to the penthouse floor."

"Thanks," she began, but he had already given her arm a little squeeze and turned away. Wow, if all the men at the hotel looked like him, she might go there again, just for the view. She watched him walk away, stopping to chat with several other patrons as he went. That was no hotel uniform he was wearing. It was tailored to fit his very cute rear end, and she stared until he went around a corner and disappeared from view. The elevators were past a row of slot machines, and she paused to put a dollar in one, for luck. She pushed the button and came up with three sevens. Fifty dollars! That was more than she had bargained for. She tucked the printed-out winning slip in her purse and faced the elevator just a few feet away.

Her lucky win giving her more confidence, she pressed the button. The doors opened and she moved to board, but back in the corner was a couple wrapped in each other's arms. The strawberry-blonde woman looked like she was about to rip her partner's clothes off, and Julia's eyes went wide. She moved back and let the doors close. After a moment, another elevator opened and she stepped in, slipping her card in the slot to send the car to the penthouse level. She used the time to draw a few deep breaths and try to calm her racing heart. The passionate lovers in the other elevator had reminded her of what she was letting herself in for.

The numbers above the door lit up in turn as the glass box rose, giving her a view of the busy casino floor below. There was still time to back out, wasn't there? The bell pinged at her floor—should she get off? Or maybe stay on the elevator, and go back to the lobby. The doors began to close again, and she reached out and held them open—if not now, when?

Overnight bag slung over one shoulder; she stepped into the penthouse hallway. There were only a few doors visible from the where she stood, and a sign on the opposite wall told her that suites 1-5 were to the left, so she took a deep breath, squared her shoulders, and marched off to meet her fate.

Chapter Two

Mark was surprised to hear a knock at the door. His one-night-stand should have her own key, so he opened the door expecting to see housekeeping, or maybe room service with the drinks he had ordered. Instead, he faced a very petite, very determined looking young woman with a hand raised as if to knock again. He took in her alluring, feminine figure, wavy brown hair around a pink-cheeked face, and wide blue eyes gazing curiously back at him.

"I take it you're not housekeeping, then?"

A pucker formed between her straight brows. "No, did you want me to be?" She jutted her chin toward him and dropped the hand that still hung in midair.

"Absolutely not," he said, looking up and down the hallway. "I had asked for some extra towels..." He trailed off, and a moment of silence stretched out while they looked at each other. When she didn't say anything, he smiled and said, "I'm Mark and you're?"

"Julia." She spoke so quietly he had to lean in to hear her.

She certainly didn't act like someone who was brazen enough to book a one-night-stand with a stranger. "Just to be sure—Madame Evangeline sent you?"

She looked up and met his eyes. "Yes. May I come in?"

"Of course, please." He stepped back to let her pass, following her with his eyes as she dropped her bag on a suitcase rack by the door and walked to the windows. She looked out, facing away from him. "Didn't you get a card key, too?"

Standing between the parted draperies, she held it up for him to see. "Yep. I just felt funny using it when you were already here."

He joined her and looked over her shoulder out the window. She froze when he stood so close behind her. That was a surprise.

The Strip lay below in all its flashing, neon glory. A faintly floral fragrance from her soft-looking hair drew his attention back to the room and the very desirable woman in front of him. Nice. He lifted a hand to touch it and then stopped, surprising himself with his hesitation. "I love the lights here."

When she turned around to face him, Mark understood why he'd held back. Julia was utterly different than the women he spent his weekends with. And it wasn't just the soft curves of her no-doubt natural breasts, or the minimal makeup on her lovely face. The slight tremble in her full, lower lip as she stood under his scrutiny. The whole package together took his breath away, and for once in his wild, playboy life, he had no idea what to say. Or how to begin.

***

Julia was stunned. She had never imagined that the guy Madame would send her would be so magazine-cover drool-worthy. He had tall, dark and handsome written all over him in letters two inches high. He was either lightly tanned or his natural skin color was a pale gold a couple of shades lighter than his amber eyes and much lighter than his hair, which was deep mahogany. Was there a crayon that color? Maybe in the sixty-four pack.

Her gaze drifted lower; she should probably be thinking about the six-pack right in front of her. Even lower, her blush crept into her cheeks again as she took in the tented front of his very nicely fitted slacks. Had pants always been so...eye catching? She hadn't even had sex one time, and yet, she was focusing on the below-the-waist assets of every man in Las Vegas! Doubts assailed her, and she forced her eyes closed. It truly was too late to back out now; if she did, she'd never try it again. The image of herself as a withered spinster, left on the shelf, never having had the guts to lie with any man imprinted itself on her closed lids and made her shudder.

Her eyes slowly came back up and up, across the broad chest and the proud chin, the full lips and to his golden eyes. The guy in the lobby was nice-looking, but she'd hit the jackpot with the hunk in front of her. Madam knew her business. She couldn't have found a sexier man if she'd built him from a kit. A virgin's dream.

"What are you thinking?"

"I—that is, I'm thinking that you're very good looking." She blew out a breath. *Smooth.*

"Thank you." His low, rumbling voice sent fingers of excitement right to her core. What did he think of her? She was curvier than was fashionable, but a compliment of some kind would be nice.

A long moment of silence drew out while they stood facing each other. Less than a foot apart physically, it seemed an uncrossable barrier stood between them. Finally, Julia couldn't stand it anymore and lifted on tiptoe to brush a soft kiss across his lips. It certainly broke the ice. He wrapped his arms around her and pulled her hips tight to his, bending to take the kiss to the next level. Julia wasn't new to kissing—she had dated, after all. And she had enough experience to know that the guy was amazingly gifted. She looped her arms around his neck and surrendered the last of her doubts.

His lips were firm and insistent. When she parted her own, he took advantage of the opening to plunder her mouth. Her world contracted to just that kiss, his nip at her lower lip, the teasing tip of his tongue stroking hers until her knees threatened to give out from the dizzying sensations. He held her firmly against him, and his hands slid down to cup her ass, strong fingers digging through her silky skirt and lifting her slightly so she was back on tiptoe, and even more off balance.

Mark pulled back, let her drop to her feet again, and looked down at her, amber eyes darkened to a deep gold and smoky with desire. Before she could wonder what he might have planned next, a knock sounded on the door followed by a voice announcing, "Room service."

When he released her, Julia grasped with both hands for the windowsill behind her and watched him go to the door to let in the waiter with a tray of drinks and a platter with a silver cover. Mark dealt with the man, his voice as cool and even as if they'd been sitting across the room from one another discussing the weather. Julia was dismayed until she saw his shoulders shake as he drew a deep breath before turning back to her. He had great self-control, but he wasn't, thank God, unaffected by their kiss.

When he turned back toward her, he was pulling his shirt over his head. The cocky smile that was revealed as he tossed the garment into a corner belied her earlier impression. But before she could carry the thought any further, he dropped his hands to his leather belt. Julia felt like a mouse playing staredown with a snake. Transfixed. Still silent, he loosened the silver-colored buckle, pulling it out through the loops, and then began to unbutton his jeans. Moving to the bed, he sat to pull off his black leather boots, stopped, and tilted his head to the side, one boot held in his hand.

"Aren't you going to undress?"

"Oh, yes, of course." She smiled and tried to look confident, but the warmth of moments before chilled. When she had signed up for this evening, she hadn't exactly been forthright. In filling out the paperwork, she had implied that her level of sexual experience was "moderate". She was afraid the service would turn her down, that maybe a virgin was unqualified for a one-night-stand under their policies.

Mark had no idea what he was dealing with, but even with her inexperience, she'd expected more seduction than this. Narrowing her eyes, she glared at him. Whether he knew it or not, it was her first time and she was *not* going to be rushed. If he didn't have the sense to make this encounter special, she'd have to provide guidance

She pasted what she hoped was a sensual smile on her face. What had he asked? Oh, yes. Would she take off her clothes. Years of fantasies surfaced, thousands of romance novels devoured, imagining her own moment of truth. "I was hoping you'd do it for me." She fluttered her eyelashes, cliché? Whatever. The gleam in his eye told her he was interested in her plan.

She turned away from him to show the row of buttons that ran all the way down her indigo blue sundress to the knee length hem. "Please? I can't reach them all."

***

Mark's mouth dried. He stood quickly and took a step toward her, stumbling over the boot he still wore. Hopping on one foot, he managed to yank it off and dropped it to the floor, never halting his forward motion.

He'd unbuttoned a few dresses before, although he couldn't remember much about them at the moment. He placed a hand on each of her hips and turned her to face him. Reaching behind her, he slipped open one after another of the tiny, fabric covered buttons. His eyes focused on her tempting, ivory throat, and he bent to press his lips against the pulse that beat there, inhaling her light, floral perfume and the underlying, spicy scent that could only be Julia.

When he'd opened the buttons to her waist, he stepped back and slipped the dress off her shoulders, revealing her white lace bra with its front hook, then her smooth, white abdomen. So feminine, he rested a hand on the softness of her slight roundness there, her skin silken and the curve doing things to his breathing that he would never have expected.

Week after week, he went out with hot women from the club scene. They were all beautiful, and not one had anything but an absolutely flat abdomen, earned through starvation and a strict workout routine. Setting her slightly away from him, he took in what he had revealed with hungry eyes. Nothing about those nearly-identical women had ever made him feel... Had ever made him feel anything except an unremarkable lust.

He pulled her close again, reached around her and opened the buttons to below her hips. With a swish, the dress slid off and fell to the floor. She followed its fall with her eyes, and when they came back up, she shuddered, just seeing him looking at her. Could she see his hunger? Her hands were still at her sides, and her eyes met his, as she stood there in her bra and very tiny white lace panties. Her breasts curved above the tops of the bra cups. Were her nipples pink or deeper, maybe coral-hued—he wanted to find out. *Now.*

He stepped back and finished unbuttoning his jeans, pushing them to the floor and stepping out of them. He wore the skintight boxer-briefs that so many women seemed to find sexy. *Does she?* They were standing only a few feet apart, but again his finesse had deserted him.

He was never hesitant in the bedroom? He slept with different women every week. Inches separated them, and he reached for her, but something in her face stopped him. Her eyes were wide and her full, lower lip trembled slightly. As did her hand, when she raised it to her cheek.

"Are you cold?" he asked. "The air conditioning is set pretty low, let me raise it."

"No." She moved her hand away from her face and rested it on his arm. "I'm not cold." Her face was tilted up toward him, and he bent to capture her lips, savoring their softness, and her intoxicating scent as he moved to close the distance between them. He reached to unhook the front of her bra and looked down between their bodies as her breasts spilled out. Satisfying his curiosity.

"Lovely." He slid his hands underneath them and cupped them in his palms. Their soft fullness caught him off guard, and he stroked their undersides with his thumbs. Most of the club girls had implants because very low body fat didn't usually equal big boobs. But Julia's silken handfuls were one hundred percent natural. Her nipples were a deep rose color that made his mouth water. Returning his gaze to her face, he saw her eyes were drooping. So sensual, so erotic. His cock pushed against his shorts, straining the fabric.

He stepped back and took her hand, tugging her toward the bed and pulling her down to sit with him on its edge. He kissed her again, softly, lifted her legs onto the mattress and piled fluffy pillows under her head.

"Julia? Are you comfortable?"

"Hmmm?" Her gaze me his, but her lids were lowered halfway and her breathing was an audible pant. "Oh, yes, very comfortable." She lifted a hand and rested it on his arm, trailing her fingernails over his wrist.

He sat on the bed, taking in his one-nighter.

She looked like a renaissance painting, all lovely colors blended together. Her brown hair with its coppery highlights that made it reflect light in a golden haze, her creamy skin. Against the hotel's indigo comforter, her eyes looked even bluer and her skin even paler. She was more vivid and more elegant than anything he'd ever seen before. And for one night, she was his.

He filled his hands with her breasts, loving their softness against his palms. He'd never realized how much he disliked hard, silicone boobs until now. Julia was a real girl.

***

Julia was a girl veering between turn-on and terror. Every touch of Mark's hand sent new sensations racing through her body. She had indeed been bare-breasted before with a man. But there was something about the way Mark touched her and looked at her that made her heart pound and her mouth dry. Probably it was because she planned to sleep with him. No-holds barred—she wanted it all. And she hadn't told Madame because she didn't want some guy who was looking for a virgin to add to his woman collection. No, she wanted an exciting evening of being treated like a woman, finally.

She rested her head among the fluffy down pillows and allowed him to take the lead. He crawled up beside her, gracefully, like a jungle cat, and lay beside her, nude. She could see his underwear on the floor by the bed. She craned her neck to try to see what she'd gotten herself in for, but the angle was wrong. *In just a few minutes, I'll be done with this virginity nonsense.* She closed her eyes tightly, fear overwhelming the desire, waiting for his next move.

"Look at me," he said, and she opened them again. "Blue like the Caribbean."

She was caught in his own amber gaze, taking in how long his lashes were and the stubble she could see on his cheek. Her fingers strayed up to touch the roughness, and she rubbed her palm across his face, liking the tingle the little hairs gave her. She wondered how it would feel against her lips, and raised her head to find out.

His rough cheek felt great, and she rubbed her lips back and forth, savoring the sensation. Why had she never taken the time to explore anyone she had been with before? She would have lost her virginity years ago. Or maybe it was just Mark. His scent drew her, something wild and spicy, cinnamon and sandalwood, and male.

He turned his head and kissed her again. Lips slightly parted, they breathed each other's breath, slow, sweet, intoxicating. The tip of his tongue stroked her lip and she sighed before timidly reaching out with her own to touch his, tangling in a complicated, erotic dance. Julia squirmed, feeling vulnerable when he parted her legs and pinned her beneath his muscular thigh.

He reached for her breasts again and began to stroke them, speaking softly. "Julia, you have the softest skin, and your nipples are so hard. I want to lick them, bite them, make you scream."

Her squirming increased. Moisture pooled between her thighs, and as he went on, she began to feel a wet spot on the bed beneath her. "Shall I do that, beautiful Julia? Do you want me to bite your nipples? Will you beg me to?"

"Oh, yes. I want you to." She thrust her chest toward him, his words wiping away her fears in a wash of desire.

"What do you want me to do? Tell me." He moved his mouth to her earlobe, nipping it with sharp teeth. "Is this it? Shall I use my teeth on your nipples too?"

"Yes, yes," she said, shuddering.

"Yes what?"

"Nip me, bite me, lick my breasts, please. I want your mouth on me."

"Where?" He gave a tug on her lobe and she felt an electric shock all the way to her toes.

"Everywhere, lick me everywhere."

He released his hold and licked slowly down her neck, making her want to squeal. "All you had to do was ask."

She opened her mouth to respond to his cocky remark, but closed it when he blew cool air on her stiffened nipples. Her blood rushed through her veins, and she felt so alive she almost forgot that she wasn't the wanton woman she was showing him.

True to his word, he laved her nipples with his hot tongue, one at a time, while pinching the other with his fingertips. She tangled her fingers in his hair, her head tossed back on the pillow and eyes squeezed very tight. He was licking slowly, taking long seconds to make each circle around her nipples, and the sweet agony of waiting for each part of her areola to be touched by that rough tongue was almost more than she could stand. Suddenly, he pulled back and looked up at her from under lowered lashes, searing her with his gaze, before dropping his head back and sucking her nipple into his mouth, biting down, just enough for the pain and pleasure to mingle and she cried out.

"Mark, God, where did you learn to do that?"

The preposterousness of her question struck her just as he chuckled. The vibration of his lips while her nipple was held tightly in his teeth sent her over the edge. She came, digging her fingers into his scalp and feeling muscle contractions all the way down to her toes. The wave went on and on, leaving her limp and gasping.

He peered up at her face. "Do you always come when someone nips you like this." He moved his mouth to her other nipple and sucked it into his mouth, biting harder this time, twisting it between his teeth.

"No. I—don't." She had never orgasmed with a man, ever. As he sucked her peak farther into his mouth, the moisture between her legs ran down onto her thighs. "Is it unusual?" Her hands left his hair to stroke across his broad shoulders. His skin felt warm, and she found herself wanting to dig her fingers into the tensed muscles at the base of his neck.

He released her nipple with a pop and pushed himself up on his elbows. "Are you serious?"

She drew a shuddering breath. *Don't give yourself away, Julia. He may not want you if he finds out how inexperienced you are.* "Yes—no, I guess not. I only know it's never happened to me before."

"Me either." His broad smile and the twinkle in his eyes captivated her, and she reached a hand to his cheek, guiding him to her kiss. He rolled to the right, taking her with him so that she was on top straddling his hips and very aware of his erection pressing at the juncture of her thighs.

Chapter Three

She was so wet. He pressed the length of his penis along her slit, moving his hips back and forth, enjoying the heat and the wide-eyed look she gave him. He'd been told he was bigger than average, was he scaring her? "Julia, is everything okay?"

Her grin reassured him. "More than okay, it's wonderful." She bent to give him a quick kiss.

"Slide forward." He put his hands under her ass cheeks, guiding her up his chest until her pussy was right in front of his face. She smelled so good, and he inhaled deeply, drawing the perfume that was Julia into his chest. If ever there was a woman he wanted to taste, it was her; and he brought her to his mouth, reaching out to lap up the juices that ran freely from her soft folds. He could hear her short pants as he teased, and when he sucked right on her clitoris, she squealed. She was so responsive, he wanted to make her come over and over just for the pleasure of listening to her.

"Mark, I want..."

What did she want? His long slow licks were apparently rendering her incoherent.

"Isn't there something I can do for you? His prick twitched in response to her incredibly sexy voice.

"I think so." He waited to see what she had in mind, his breathing growing ragged when she turned, facing away from him and wrapping one silken hand around the base of his rigid staff. He was only human and the things he'd been doing to her had been making him hotter and harder by the minute. Her little hand was almost too much, and he tried to distract himself. Although the view of her neatly shaved, almost hairless pussy was not helping to distract him at all. He shuddered and buried his face in her once again, wallowing in the scents and the sounds she made when his tongue stroked directly on her swollen clit. A squeal from the back of her throat vibrated her mouth over his penis and told him more about her state than almost anything else.

He continued to lap up her juices, but he struggled to concentrate because she had moved her hand to his balls and stroked them, and her lips covered the head of his cock, slipping down over its length, so slowly, getting even for his little nipple game, he supposed. It was torture, as each fraction of an inch of skin was covered by her hot little mouth. Not moving back and forth, almost no motion at all, just a slow engulfing of his prick. He almost stopped breathing when he felt its engorged head touch the back of her throat.

And she stayed like that, for long seconds. The woman was a witch, her cock-sucking technique different than any he'd ever felt before. Just as he thought he might explode right there, she moved, sliding back up so that only the head was in her mouth. She ran her tongue around it in slow circles.

He wrapped his arms around her hips, pulling her right against his face, and began to lick in earnest, fast strokes from front, all the way to her sweet little ass. Fast so that she would speed up, maybe meet his rhythm and ease the torment he felt. So she would pick up on his cue and they could reach their peaks together. He wanted to shoot his load down that beautiful throat, and he bucked his hips. But nothing he did made her change her slow, maddening rhythm.

He turned his head to the side. "Julia, faster, please, I can't stand it. Suck my cock, come on, baby. Ah, hell." He couldn't wait any longer to fuck that beautiful pussy. "Come here." He flopped her beside him on the bed and turned her around so they were lying side by side.

"Come on, Julia." He pushed her legs apart and slipped one finger into her sopping pussy, then two. "You're so ready for me, baby. I'm gonna fuck your brains out. You'll like that, won't you, baby? Tell me you want me to fuck you." He grabbed for a foil packet on the bedside table and tore it open with his teeth, rolling the condom onto his rigid staff.

Her voice broke on a sob, but she said, "I do, I want to feel you inside me, go ahead, fuck my brains out. It's why we're here, after all."

The very tiny part of his brain that wasn't completely controlled by his lust registered that her comment was an odd thing to say, but it was, after all, a miniscule part of his personality. The rest was tied up in the getting his penis inside that welcoming snatch. He propped himself up on his arms, looking down at her intent face, eyes closed again.

"Open your eyes, beautiful. I want to watch your face while I fuck you. Come, on, Julia...Julia are you okay?"

***

She was more than okay. She was completely blown away by the whole experience. But she was a little scared as she felt the large, bulbous head of his penis brush against her entrance. He murmured nonsense syllables against her neck and she opened her eyes as he moved his head back. He wanted to watch her face, and she wasn't sure she was a good enough actress to hide her fear and anticipation of an act that had taken long enough to arrive.

She felt her channel stretching as he pushed in, pushing against that barrier that he didn't know was there. But she did and she felt a sharp pain and gasped as he pushed through the bit of skin that blocked him from fully entering her. He held her gaze with his golden, amber cat's eyes, and Julia was hypnotized. The pain passed, replaced by a sharp wash of pleasure, and she wrapped her legs around his thighs, and her arms around his neck, holding on for the ride of her life. She held her eyes closed for just a couple of seconds, taking it all, taking him in, and when she opened them again, she saw him staring down at her in what looked like horror.

"Julia, dear God, you're not, that is—you were a virgin, weren't you?"

"Yes," her voice was so low even she could barely hear it. But it was pointless to deny what they both knew was the truth. "I was."

He froze, only part of his cock inside her, but her tight passage held it in place. "Then why?"

She lifted her hips and felt him slide deeper. "Just fuck me, Mark. Fuck now, talk later because I'm not interested in a conversation—just now."

And apparently he had no compunction in following her instructions because he surged forward and buried himself to the hilt, drawing a moan from her very core. She had waited so long to feel the ecstasy of a man filling her with his rigid cock and it was more than she'd ever expected.

***

For a moment he'd faltered. A virgin? On a one-night-stand? But when she'd held him in place, welcomed him, he hadn't been able to think beyond how warm she felt around him, how wet. How incredible it felt to slide his engorged length into her tight, hot pussy. He couldn't help himself, couldn't stop.

Questions could be answered later, at the moment all he wanted was the friction that was rapidly sending him to places he didn't remember ever visiting before. Stars swam before his eyes when he squeezed them closed. He wanted to stop, wanted to find out why she had spent her virginity in a one-night encounter in a strange city, but his body fought him when he tried. His body demanded he continue. She begged him to go on, holding him tightly against her and meeting his every thrust with her own. In fact, he was extremely turned on being her first, just as he'd loved the feel of her natural breasts and the little curve of her belly.

"Come for me, Julia, can you do that, baby?" He was trying to maintain a rhythm, to keep stroking until she found her release before spilling his seed, but she wasn't quite there, and it was a supreme battle to hold it back. "Julia, are you close?"

Her answer was a long wail and a series of rippling contractions in the passage that held his penis. It threw him over the edge into orgasm, balls tightening and hot liquid shooting from the end of his cock, the two of them bucking and writhing until the endless ecstasy faded slowly back, leaving him skin to skin against the sexiest woman he had ever known.

He rolled to the side, not wanting to crush her under his greater weight, and through half-closed lids, surveyed Julia's sweat-glistening form. Her creamy skin caught the lamp's light and he lifted his hand to trace the outline of a full breast, just touching the edge of her rose pink nipple and watching it peak instantly. He cupped its fullness, so soft, so feminine, and let his hand run down her belly, its slight roundness astoundingly sensual. His breath had slowed to nearly normal, and he had to ask....

"Why, Julia?"

Chapter Four

S he had known the moment would come. It was a logical question, and her once reasonable plan for eliminating an inconvenient hymen didn't seem to pertain anymore. How was she to have known what an incredible moment it would be, the joining of two bodies, two spirits. *Damn it.*

"I didn't know it would be like this. I just kind of felt like life was leaving me behind. I was afraid to go on dates because with everyone I had to question whether to go this far, whether to make him 'the one' and it was making me crazy."

"Most girls I've met gave it up when they were teenagers." He shook his head. "I am pretty sure you're the oldest virgin I've ever met."

"Gee, thanks." She grinned, too full of after-glow to get mad, despite the feeling that she should be insulted.

"No, you know what I mean. I just don't know what to think."

"Me either. Particularly after the last couple of hours. I've been missing out."

He grinned. "Thank you."

"You're welcome." She giggled. "How polite we are. I specifically asked for a playboy type, a guy who dated a different girl every week, so he would be experienced, but I probably wouldn't like him that much. And look who they sent me! Madame has a lot to answer for, sending me a sweet guy like you. And incredibly talented. Oh, that feels good."

He was running light fingers up and down her arm, just barely touching her. But it sent chills down her spine. "You know, I feel like I could use a shower."

"Oh, go ahead." She pulled her arm in to her body. "I'll take one too before we leave." It was over, but she was going to be brave. She'd gotten what she came for, and probably a lot more than she paid for, too. She shouldn't be greedy and hope for more....

He slid off the edge of the bed and held out his hand. "Don't you want to take one together? This room has an incredible shower with jets all over the place. I looked when I first came in."

More! "Oh, yes, that sounds great. I've always wanted to try a shower like that." As he quirked an eyebrow at her with a wicked grin on his full, sensuous lips, she smiled back. "But I think you have more than cleanliness in mind."

Chapter Five

He took her hand and pulled her with him toward the bathroom. "Come with me, Miss Innocent, and I'll show you what I can do for you with all those streaming jets."

Her breath caught. His naked body in the lamplight was sculpture. As if carved from warm, living marble, every plane and angle pleasing to her eye. She allowed him to lead her into the bathroom and stood back while he turned on the shower and adjusted the temperature and jets. As he moved, she watched his muscles flexing under his skin. In this brighter light his olive-toned skin was perfection. Apparently there was no light that wasn't perfect for Mark. The rear view was amazing and before she knew it, she had reached out and put one hand on each of his ass cheeks, digging her nails in slightly. God, was he built.

"Like what you see?" His chuckle was low and vibrated up her arms.

"That's what did it." Her blood sang in her veins. She wanted him again, immediately. And what did he have planned for that shower with its inviting bench on either end?

He looked at her over his shoulder then turned to face her. My, he was happy to see her again. His cock jutted straight out from his body, already completely hard and there was a drop of liquid on the tip. She reached out a tentative finger to touch it, smoothing it around the head of his penis, then putting her finger in her mouth.

He stared, and she wondered if she'd done something wrong, but he pulled her against him and put his mouth at her ear, warm breath caressing her skin. "That's what did what?"

"Huh?" She was lost.

"You said, 'That's what did it.' What did you mean?"

Her mind was blank for a moment. What had she said? Oh, yes, a thought came through the murk. "I meant, when you chuckled, that deep sound, with your mouth on my nipple, that's what made me come the first time."

"Really? I'm intrigued. I wonder where else I could put my mouth and do that...."

Her eyes widened, and she forgot to breathe. "I can think of a place," she said, surprising herself with her quick response.

"Mmm," he nuzzled her neck. "And we'll do that, beautiful, but first let's see what the shower is like."

She followed him into the shower. It was as big as her entire bathroom at home and had at least a dozen jets shooting water into the center. There was a dispenser on the wall filled with a liquid soap/shampoo and he reached over and filled his hands with the slippery substance, rubbing them together to create a green-apple scented foam.

"Turn around." The bubbles were spilling between his fingers, and she faced the back wall, resting her hands on its white-tiled surface. He put his palms against her upper back and began to wash her in big circles, the foam slipping down and running between her butt cheeks. When she trembled, he asked, "Do you like that?" He dropped to his knees and continued to rub the foam down her back until his fingers caressed her ass.

His fingertips moved between her cheeks, caressing just the very top of her crack, and though she tensed, waiting for him to reach further, to her aching pussy, he just continued to wash down her legs to her feet. He stayed on his knees and gave her a little push. "Sit."

He was getting pretty demanding. She liked it though—she liked it a lot. She wasn't sure what that said about her, but having a hot guy tell her what to do naked was working for her big time. She sat on the bench and he picked up one of her feet.

***

The shower jets hit all over his body as he knelt on the shower floor, but it felt good, incredible really. And he was so involved with touching every inch of Julia's skin, that he only noticed the spray in a secondary kind of way.

He pumped more soap into his palm, and lifting one of her feet, ran his soapy hands over its top and her arch, between her toes. Her nails were painted a rose pink, so close to the color of her nipples, he thought absently, casting his eyes toward those stiff peaks above him. He held the foot and let the shower jets wash away the soapy foam, then ran his hands slowly up her calves and thighs, massaging gently and loving the feel of her soft skin under his hands. He knew his own skin was rough, but she didn't complain. In fact, when he looked up at her face, her eyes were half-closed and looking down at him, their blue barely showing through her lashes. He went for the other foot, slowly washing that one and moving up her leg.

"Open your legs for me." She parted them and he reached up with sudsy fingers and saw the tinge of blood on her inner thigh. He traced it with a slick fingertip. A virgin! He wouldn't have agreed to meet her if he'd known. But he would have missed out on the best night he'd had in a long time. Maybe ever.

Although she lifted her hips, and he knew what she wanted, he continued his leisurely washing of her lovely, soft skin, running his hands over the curve of belly and on to the breasts he couldn't keep away from. Silicone was highly overrated. Soft, natural breasts like Julia's were definitely the way to go.

Suddenly, the quiet, the lack of conversation made him nervous. The only sound was the hissing of the water jets and their breathing. Julia was more than the body he had become obsessed with. He wanted to know what she was thinking, feeling. That was a new idea for Mark the playboy.

"Julia?"

"Hmmm?"

Shit, he had to think of something to ask her, and he didn't know what he wanted. He wanted to hear her voice.

"Is the water warm enough?"

***

Her eyelids fluttered open. "What? Yes, oh, yes it's fine." It was hard to form words, for some reason. Every bit of her attention was focused on following his hands as they soaped and explored her body. He was washing her arms, soaping from her shoulders down to her fingertips, and she felt completely boneless. Boneless but tingling.

"Okay, I just wanted to make sure you were okay. You're so quiet."

"Oh, sorry." *Was that the right thing to say?* Damn her inexperience. Between the water hissing and her heart pounding in her ears, the shower stall seemed pretty loud to her.

He pumped some more soap into his hand and sank down onto the bench beside her. "I want to wash your hair." She turned away and he massaged the shampoo into her hair, then took a moveable showerhead off its hook and rinsed it away.

"I think I'm pretty clean," she said. "Or at least most of me."

His eyes met hers, and he smiled. "I saved the best for last."

"Well, I think you will have to wait."

He frowned and she grinned, feeling more confident in the face of his chagrin. "I think only one of us is clean. Stand up."

He obediently stood in front of her. This put one of his more interesting assets right at her face level and she took a moment to look more closely at his cock. It jutted toward her face, and she decided to tease just a little and took the head into her mouth, licking around twice before releasing it.

"No, don't stop," he said, reaching out for her, but she shrugged under his arms and stood up.

"Sorry, I'd love to keep going, but I don't want to be accused of slacking. You just spent a very long time washing me and now it's my turn." The look on his face was priceless. Powerful stuff, this sexuality was, and she began to realize that and enjoy it. She followed the same path he had, back first, then legs and feet and up the front. Skipping the one area she knew he wanted touched the most. Turn about was definitely fair play—and fun, too.

But besides that, she found that running her soapy hands over his body was incredible in itself. The play of muscles under his skin, the coarse hair on his legs, she was learning as she went and paying very close attention to his reactions. When she pinched one of his dark-apricot guy nipples, his dick jerked and bumped against her stomach. *Interesting*.

But by the time she was done with all but the most interesting parts, his patience seemed to be thinning. She soaped her hand and ran it between her legs, then over his rock-hard cock.

"Julia!"

She fought to contain her giggles at the strain in his voice. "Yes?"

"Enough, I can't stand it. Come here." He pulled her against him, pressing that hard cock back into her belly. "I want you now."

"Oh, sure. Now that we're clean and all."

He glared at her and she let her giggles free. "You spent a very long time torturing me with those talented fingers of yours. I just wanted to repay the favor."

"It's not funny," he said, but the corner of his

mouth twitched. He shifted her in his arms so they were kissing, streams of water hitting them from all around. He was no longer behaving as though he had all day, but was urgently prying her mouth open and ravishing it. When her tongue tangled with his, he shifted his hands down to her ass and lifted her so that her feet were off the floor. He braced his hands under her thighs and pressed her back against the shower wall.

She gasped and he broke the kiss to look down at her. "What's wrong?"

She pointed and he looked down to see he had placed her so that one of the jets was shooting directly against her clitoris.

"Oh, no." He made as though to move her away, but she punched his shoulder.

"No, don't move, it's so...it's so...."

"Good?" He held her in place as her body shuddered and she clung to his shoulders.

"I really need to remodel my bathroom," she said, holding tight until the world stopped spinning.

Before she could do anything else, he lifted her slightly and drove his cock into her quaking passage. "I can't wait any more." He slammed it in, two or three times, then slowed, gliding in and out, over and over, so that his tip hit a place inside her she had only read about.

"Yes, Julia, there is a G-spot," she murmured into his neck and then screamed his name as she came again. "Mark, oh God, yes, yes."

He shuddered as he spilled inside her, finding his own release yet again. "I can't even believe how tight you are, Julia!" He held her up with her legs wrapped around his waist for another moment, then collapsed with her on his lap onto one of the benches. Water streamed over them, hitting from all angles, and suddenly the heat, the water beating against her skin, the steam became overwhelming

"Mark, please turn it off. I can't stand it."

He reached over and turned off the shower. "Are you okay? I should have thought—it was your first time. You're sore, aren't you. I'm so sorry."

She shook her head then laid it against his shoulder. "It's not that, I'm not sore. It's just that all of a sudden it was like sensory overload. Good, bad, intense. I didn't know what to do with myself."

He laid his head back against the wall. "Oh, that I understand. Let's get out of here and get dry. I think I might need to lie down for a bit. What a workout."

She dropped a kiss on his neck and stood on shaky legs. "Okay, I think I might be able to make it that far. Stepping out of the shower, she handed him a towel and tucked one around herself, wrapping another around her hair. "So, that's what everyone's been talking about," she said, shaking her head. "I can't believe I waited this long to find out."

Chapter Six

Towel around his waist, he followed her out of the bathroom. "Julia, that's not, I mean, tonight is not what everyone is talking about. I've been just the playboy you asked for, a different silicone babe every week, and I can assure you, it's never been like this."

She tilted her head and looked at him. "I'm sure you're right. I couldn't possibly keep up with girls like that."

"That is not what I mean. Those girls, I don't know how to explain the difference, but they aren't like you. You're real, every soft, curvy, cuddly, exciting inch of you. Not one of them could keep up with you." He hoped she understood how extraordinary she was, but was afraid his poor words weren't carrying it well enough.

She smiled at him. "I had a good teacher. But prof, I'm awfully sleepy. Do you think we could lie down for a while?" She undid the towel in her hair and unwrapped the one around her body. "I should find my bag. I brought a sexy nightie to sleep in."

He held out his hand and took the two towels

from her, tossing them, and his, into the bathroom. "Don't get the nightie. Just come curl up with me and we'll take a nap. It's been quite a night."

She yawned then looked startled. "I completely forgot you ordered the drinks. And what is on the covered dish?"

"If you like, I'll pour us some champagne."

"I'm awfully sleepy...what's in the dish?"

"Take a look and see if it's anything you like."

She stretched her arms over her head and walked over to the table. "I don't know, I think I'm too tired to...strawberries! Strawberries with brown sugar and sour cream. Oh, I'm hungry. Go ahead and open the champagne--I just got a second wind."

She carried the plate with its booty over to the bed and plopped down cross-legged against the headboard. "How did you know?"

"I didn't. Madame said there would be refreshments in the room. I've never seen strawberries with sour cream before."

"I had it at a party once and fell in love." She took a big, red strawberry dipped it in the cream and then the sugar. Dark gold crystals clung to the sides of the berry. "Taste." She took a glass of champagne from him and held the treat up for him to bite. She was so delighted, he didn't want to say no.

He chewed and swallowed, closing his eyes as the sweetness of the sugar and the tart sour cream collided with the rich berry juice in his mouth. "That is amazing." He sat down on the edge of the bed next to her and smiled. "Who would have thought?"

"I don't know, somebody very smart." She finished the first berry and dipped another, offering it to him. He looked at her, sitting cross-legged and naked on the bed, holding up the red fruit with its sugary coating. A one-night-stand. And Mark, who had one-night-stands several times a month, felt melancholy flutter its wings around his heart. Someone was going to be very lucky when this woman decided who she wanted forever. But it was going to have to be someone better than him. He didn't deserve her, and he wasn't kidding himself that he did.

Enough. He drew a deep breath. He had her for one night.

Julia sighed and pushed the nearly empty plate away. The champagne flute she put on the bedside table, and she slid down and curled onto her side. "I need to close my eyes, just for a minute." Mark lay down behind her, spooning her and wrapping an arm around her waist. He tugged her closer as her limbs softened and her breaths became long and even. Quite some time passed before he joined her in sleep, his mind moving over possibilities, ideas foreign to his playboy mentality. One night with Julia was not going to be enough.

Chapter Seven

She woke with a start, for a moment panicked. Where was she—then she remembered. The arm across her waist was a clue. *Mark*. Her one-night-stand. But through the open drapes she could see a fine line of light along the eastern horizon. Daytime was coming and with it, reality.

She slipped out of the bed and padded to the window. Las Vegas lay below, still flashing its lights for her admiration, but she knew the sun would be up soon, and it was time for her to go. She grabbed her overnight bag and slipped into the bathroom to dress.

When she came out a few minutes later, the sky was noticeably lighter. She set her bag down and pulled the heavy drapes closed. No reason for Mark to have to wake up early so far as she knew. He was draped across the bed, arms spread wide and a slight smile on his face. She hoped he was having a good dream. She paused for a moment by the desk.

Julia leaned over the bed and pressed a very soft kiss on his bristly cheek. "Don't forget me," she said, almost under her breath. "I sure won't forget you."

She slipped out of the room and rang for the elevator. If that couple from the night before was still there, she would get on anyway. Her newly advanced level of sophistication would carry her through.

***

He slept until ten. That was the time on the small clock on the bedside table when he opened his eyes. Stretching, he sat up and looked around. He couldn't remember the last time he'd slept so well. The hotel bed was luxury itself. Oh, and the little encounter last night didn't hurt either. Speaking of which...where was she?

"Julia?" There was no answer, and he had actually known there wouldn't be. It was a one-night-stand and the night was over. He'd met the one woman who could reach out and touch his heart without even trying, and she was gone.

Sighing, he stood and stepped into his boxers and jeans. He couldn't face the shower again, not after making love to her beneath the jets. He reached into his bag for his socks, found a folded piece of paper and smoothed it out on his lap. "Dear Mark," the note began. "I hope I'm not breaking the rules of 1NightStand by doing this but I wanted you to know how to reach me..." A grin spread across his face as he tucked it into his pocket.

About the Author

USA Today Bestselling Author Kate Richards is a multi-published author of spicy romance stories in various subgenres. She lives in sunny Southern California with her wonderful husband and menagerie of rescued pets.

Kate loves the beaches, mountains and deserts of her home state as well as traveling whenever possible to meet readers and other authors.

Exploring all types of relationships in her books, Kate writes menage, BDSM, and every other kind of romance she can think of.

* 9 7 8 1 6 8 3 6 1 1 0 5 9 *